At The Bottom
Of The Big Top

Words and Pictures

by

Eric C. Harrison

2006

Marsh Paw Press

2012

At The Bottom Of The Big Top
Special Edition Paperback
Words & Pictures by Eric C. Harrison

ISBN #978-0-9888040-0-5

At the Bottom of The Big Top was originally self-published "at home" in 2006 as a limited edition staple-bound chapbook. This was the first thing produced with the *Marsh Paw Press* name and logo. 20 copies were printed and distributed. This version is very slightly expanded upon and even more slightly revised. It also includes additional artwork and improved reproductions of the original artwork. This special edition also includes the original long poem "One Dead Marmoset" – which I'd intended to shorten, but ended up expanding into this collection of poems.

Write to The author at - stilldiseased@aol.com

Published by
Marsh Paw Press
2012

Big Top

Origin:
1890–95, Americanism

— n
1. the main tent of a circus
2. the circus itself

Slang
n.
a circus tent; the circus, in general. : And now,
one of the greatest acts under the big top.

mod.
having to do with the circus. : One big top
experience is enough to last me a lifetime.

The main tent of a circus, as in The high-wire
act is almost always in the big top .
[c. 1840]

Underworld slang for
a maximum-security prison.
[1950s]

At The Bottom

Of The Big Top

Poetry-Fiction

sort of a story

told with poems

Table of Contents
(sans illustrations, musical cues and any other ligaments)

Admit One

seven deadly demons send
enchanted temptations in the form of scents
to snake across carnival concourse
through auto packed dirt lot
toward eager noses

winged serpent wisps of hypnotic mixture;
hamburger-hot-dog- fried-dough aromas
Hog-Calls to wild packs of gluttonous pig-people
dazzled by the midway's colored light's dapple

from rows of candy and rainbow bulbs
subliminal sales pitch strobes between
Autumn trees silhouetted beneath
red basket seats illuminated
under pulse of beacon
on amnesty's architecture
the Ferris wheel's girders
in skeletal skyward stretch

relays downward
message of bright sights
for eyes inside autos
a trigger that heightens
pang for amusement

bane-bait to draw
the passer-by from days
of dull routine, doldrums
toward banners that wave

multi-colored magnets
boast of rides for thrill-
seekers with long faces
that will only get longer
- in long, long lines

as they wait to buy
tickets that ADMIT
ONE - BEYOND
the yellow, metal pipe-barriers

the promise of satisfaction
calls to suburbia's slaves
who possess paper presidents
and feel the burn in their pockets

"They're The easiest bait."

Screwtape, a Devil, may have
told a demon
named Wormwood

"To create CHAOS among sinners -
when they palm hot coin

is to shoot flounder in a barrel -
point blank
with a rocket launcher."

***Cue music:** TA RA RA BOOM DE AY*
Asher Moor King Morton,1892

the un-merry go 'round

carousel touched by evil spins;

work of metal and painted wood
colors blur in momentum

thrown off center, axis topples
wobbles amok, out of control

tarnished rings of brass that hold
wishes unfulfilled, roll into sewers

lost forever, submerged in sludge

ride's lights flicker as cables pull free
girders and cross-supports snap like old bones

tree born mustangs seem alive, rabid
froth at the mouth, foam through teeth

in tight clenched grind
beneath desperate, bloodshot eyes

palominos depicted forever in hateful
expressions that mirror their creators

around and around; the goldfish stampede
eternally impaled upon spine-pole prisons

night-mares rise from circular base
floorboards splinter and pulled up nails yield

liberated mock-hooves break free but cannot gallop
in accidental exodus from life like sour karma

a taunt that tortures time itself
- this torment of circular ups and downs

band organ warbles in haunting discordance
Wurlitzer's OOM!-PA!-PA! slows to a dirge

un-level cogs grind un-oiled gears
Old Man Engine
    sputters, fails

    puffs one last,
    black, smoky breath

    carny-captain abandons ship

The Doctor

away from foot-flow, carnival traffic
covered wagon hides illegal

bottles of Doctor Good that sit
with cork-stopped flasks of juju snake oil
on shelves where mason jar prisons hold

animal anomalies, deformed fetuses
manmade aberrations that appear to sleep
preserved for years in clouded liquid

dusty, cheap wood frames present
mail-order degrees hung by sketchy certificates

2 black and white photos show 4 breasted women
they smile seductively, behind glass - cracked and dirty

Bosch monstrosities paper walls
display demon faces which mirror assortment
of posters and handbills that advertise freaks
created by mad doctor, beer swilling, con-surgeon

narcotic alchemist belches out orders
to shadow, he hollers - "Get me a drink ...
... fix me a shot! " snaps off the latex

accepts tonight's failure as noble attempt
to save one who died with the truth of what was
badly botched, back room, bare-bulb rhinoplasty

Killed the fucker right
there - on the table

Time of death; five-twelve, announced
in slurred speech that rides
tell-tale odors exhaled
each breath shares evidence of Cuban cigars

pussy and bourbon, night's tale of debauchery
short history written in rank halitosis

alcoholic daydreams take
tragic backlash, memory strikes

him; "The world ... completes its circle
to become karma itself" he thinks, pictures

Rhinoceros theft, nonfatal surgery
horn slips into black medical bag
images of airplane tickets, carrion luggage

briefcases opened reveal stacks of bills
offshore bank accounts, black market cash
deal done silent, behind closed curtains

handkerchief over curved conical shape

drips crimson cost while fetching green profit
golden ticket scores more than chocolate

modern day Frankenstein-Moreau
tenders tatterdemalion, stitch-things
garden of home-spun freaks kept alive
supported, sustained with medicinal magic
orphans of science and elder witchcraft
lab grown pet abominations

(The Doctor, continued)

penned and reared by hand that profits
embittered by pain and humiliation

distorted, deformities gather outside
an angry lynch mob with torches that touch

doctor's wagon-office, turn it into a pyre
behind its wood walls bottles burst

brakes released by six fingered hand
orange kamikaze soars

flames fed by breeze of downhill momentum
leave grass fire trails
like the tails of comets

these lines of light chase fate toward Big Top

inside mobile coffin
doc writes one last RX
sure as shit remedy for today's fatal ailment

pistol finds temple,
trigger sends lead
through brain behind eyes

his vision stops

Cue music: *Stars & Stripes Forever,*
John Philip Sousa - X-mas day 1896

Ignition Intermission

tarpaulin waterproofed; heat-kissing
mixture of gasoline and paraffin wax
tickled by the tiniest spark ignites

orange and yellow bat wing fires
change to blue tongues
devour what's lapped at

***

Cue sound: *Recorded monotone voice*
comes from dime-toss
game toppled over in scuffle:

"A dime a dime, it's ONLY a dime!

A dime in the red circle
wins any small prize from the first row.

A quarter in the red circle
wins our special JUMBO prize !!!

A dime a dime,

It's Only a Dime!"

Onslaught

As the doctor's career careens,
sets Big-Top ablaze,
freaks see their chance

to seize the day. Primal
rage sets in. Signals
in malformed brains call
inner beasts to destroy

The Normals.
The most delicious dish of all;

                              revenge against the envied,

faces - smooth formed
pretty girls and handsome men
to tear apart with dirty fingers

- a senseless end to what they covet

 what un-people want.

***

hanky pank# 462

*half-inflated multi-colored balloons tacked loosely
to angled board - dull dart target; hit rarely burst
due to lack of membrane sensitivity; when popped
winner gains cheap trinket turned out by hungry
malnourished gray babies of 3rd world sweatshops*

* **Cue Music:** *Gypsies Tramps and Thieves, Cher -1970-71*

reproduced on a handsome
167f roll driven carousel
punk band organ
with marching bass boom bash

terrifying tympani beater
scary snare drum
spinal tap & roll
cymbal car crash
& corpse twitch rhythm

Bermuda triangle tingles
timed with creepy
calm-killing castanets

43 reed calliope pipes
that preach back-wood gadget gospel

backed by a 27 note glockenspiel choir

beautiful clockwork, gargantuan gizmo
6 feet tall
9 feet wide
3 feet deep
350 pounds

towed by 30 trained poodles in frill

Ambulatory Underclass

alcoholics, chain smokers, junkies, sex fiends
drugstore cowboys, pill poppers, tokers

pick pockets, con-men, neurotics, psychotics
rodeo flunkies - inept with lasso

exiles, pigs, sticky fingered cutthroats
Killers, ex-con's, creatures of bad habit

charlatans, grifters, arthritic ticket punchers
rejects, robbers, 3 card Monty masters

MDMA dabbling candy apple dippers
coke snorting clowns with facial amnesia

half-crippled contortionists, pot head road hands
versatile experts in appetite satisfaction

smooth talking dart and ball distribution diplomats
freaks we don't hear of like Andre Anaconda Dick
and his private services to ladies of high status

union of the mobile money maker
just another mule
born to chase
the income carrot dangled
in lost faces of the ambulatory underclass

road-bound outcasts of the country
with steady cross hairs on the marks

sub-culture set out to entertain
comes together in times of crisis

attacks like packs of Tasmanian badgers
in times perceived as a threat to their community

Cue music: Pig in a Blanket
                The Rudimentary Peni, 1983
In the Midst

confused, ring master caught
in shuffle spins. arms and mind akimbo
shot and killed with small clown from cannon

darkness and motion fill canvas, cavernous
lung of Big-Top - it breathes foul
putrescent air produced
by bodies that writhe as if newborn
maggots behind thin, membranous walls

animals escape in the midst of confusion
elephants trample crooked vendors and kiosks
jumbos crush stale popcorn and leaky balloons
mammoths remember Lil' Tyke and attack
trunks swing to break ribs, dulled tusks impale
feet pound and send ripples through fresh pools of blood

monkeys loot peanuts, tear apart cotton candy
sellers who peddle pink fiberglass tufts

lions and tigers follow clothed dancing grizzly
mammals maul vulnerable; screaming children

slow moving, elderly folks clutch at their chests
drop canes, spit false teeth as beast's jaws sink in

black-market black bears dance through 3 ring buffet
self-serve a gluttonous feast of sweet revenge

once shackled and caged, now on top of the chain
enormous striped cat chokes to death on pace maker

king of the jungle shows disgusted expression
roars out his dislike of the taste of prosthetics

The Last Words of Pitch and Dunk Pete

Hey, Lady !

    I heard you

        tell your friend

            you lost some weight"

                He points
                a long, bony
                finger
                at her ass

                and then shout's

                "THERE it is!"

                S P L A S H ! ! ! ! ! !

***Cue music:** Flight of The Bumblebee*
Nikolai Andreyevich Rimsky-Korsakov 1899-1890

Storm troopers of the Circus

army of old-school clowns laugh mad
some toss hatchets, others bear seltzer
bottles spray acid, arsenic, bleach

White Face warriors patrol on unicycle
tote M16 and UZI-style squirt guns
aimed at eyes, shoot lye, blind innocent

crowd of bystanders; spectators in outcry
smother under odors of chemicals and popcorn
on the rise among sounds of sizzling skin

one thousand more bozos don polka dotted uniforms
tap oversized shoes, honk red rubber nose jobs
bitter madmen, screwed by life, sport comedic war paint

Happy Hobos in grease-pen masks that cover evil frowns
pour out, by the hundreds as mini-tanks with tiny turrets
produce small flags on sticks marked: B A N G ! or BOOM !

Sad Tramp storm troopers drift
down on patchwork parachutes

dump buckets of razor blade
confetti into shrieking people

clouds of shimmering silver moths
shred skin from frightened faces

***Cue Music:** Pinhead, the Ramones - 1976*

The Side-Show Freaks will be Freaks

battle cry comes from pitchman general
in time of riot stands ten feet tall
wears bowler hat, two bit suit
cheap chain pocket watch
socks - mismatched, soup-
stained shirt, powerful

lungs demand
respect, wide stretched
mouth commands
lost, misshapen misfits to even the score
against The Normals,
        the pretties;
        the bland.

denizens of dime museums;
call to mind Halloween masks
under orange arc sodium lantern
light on streets
through bare October trees

elite sideshow unit strikes with stealth
up from under grandstand behind
bleachers - where animal shit is swept;

freaks smoke pot in that piss
-saturated, hay-strewn place
where none can smell sweet leaf's smoke
or the perpetual pungent breath expelled
by those that tip little brown
jugs marked X X X

(The Side-Show Freaks will be freaks cont.)

now they come (Tod Browning people)
out of hiding; drunk, stoned, wired
facial features distorted, twist out
expressions that spell a craving for hate

held for years; a grudge undying
like white versus black
or dog folk versus cat folk

mishaps attack with dirty sharp blades
everyone knows that freaks always carry
knives (usually a poniard, switchblade or sword-cane)

Myrna the mule faced mama steals kisses
hugs violently, clutches at men as they flee
as Laura the lizard lady snatches
one boy ... slips
two foot tongue down unwilling throat

A worthy contortionist (name unknown) hides
within the confines of a tacky leather Gucci
filled with delusions of grandeur, compressed
inside, becomes a quick snack for The Human Crocodile
who swallows the bag whole - both body and legacy
victims of circumstance ... and digestion

Efreet, the two headed boy; top secret
bio-cultivated behind closed doors
from which he charges, hat box in hand
that contains a shriveled, shrunken heirloom
the one eyed head of his uncle, The Cyclops

fake Bearded "Lady"
a bulge in his/her pants
bumps his/her ugly
old man as he eats fire

their fame - goes up in smoke;
as his/her charred chin smolders
he/she backs into
Sword Swallower (ex-whore)
who shows off
slips and guts
        herself

        falls hard
        face down
            blade up
            ass open;
                      a WHY? incision

Jo-Jo the dog-faced boy becomes
the doggy-style freak who'd watched her
swallow swords too many times
loses self
restraint thinned
by too many years
            on this day
            he decides
            he is getting
            a piece of action

before flesh gets cold
jumps on for a ride
lands on the blade
for a fuck is impaled
        with one last howl at the faraway moon
                "Gabba-Gabba Hey!"

Cue music: Anvil of Crom,
Basil Poledouris - 1982

Unbridled

fancy horse shakes off feathered bridle
trick rides in unclear fear-altered state

gallops fast with no regard
for half naked beauty fixed to its mane
bareback proves treacherous ... deadly, insane

she screams STOP!
but is tossed
bucked off,

a discarded rag-doll bleeds
caught under hooves
torn and tattered, trampled, stomped
rearranged by gravity
weight and impact
glitter and glamour introduced to gore
then she's off the bill, forever more

out of control bloodlust boils
steed recalls beat of the crop
exhales hot breath
spits rough labored neigh
leaps onto spectators, murderous, angry

heavy stones dropped onto sun gray twigs
shod feet batter bones beneath
crushing pounds pinpointed for power
within U-shaped metal once ingots
born atop black anvil
mothers under force
of hard swung hammers
spray of blood, sweat and sparks

*Cue music: *Die Walküre: Ride of the Valkyries*
R. Wagner, 1856

Death from Above

in alliance with gravity, balance and time - aerialists dive

onto traffic jam of heads at a momentary standstill, down
far below, skulls under skin crush like wet, ripe honeydews

with the greatest of ease beneath weight of human body
bombs that drop from high wires and swing free of trapeze

as indifferent to pain inflicted as one might expect
from men whose testicles have been flattened by spandex

Cause & Reaction

***Cue Music:** I Feel The Earth Move, by Carol King, 1971*

1. Earth

one miserable freak, named Earth
bumbles, in
an afternoon drunk-
en maudlin state; teeter
-totters out from behind flaps
custom embroidered "private / no trespass"

his head; a medicine ball
colorfully tattooed; world
maps; globe of flesh, bone
curiosity used as golden gimmick.

inside he feels like a blue
ribbon gourd that ranks
high upon vines
tucked among the estranged
prestigious fairground anomalies
 .
body covered
in dragons, pretty
ladies, unknown
letters, strange
symbols, memoirs
with meanings long
forgotten to priests
whose ancestors scrawled
secrets unknown to
fools who donate
their bodies turned quilt
onto which are rendered
stories, stitched
forever in ink;
hieroglyphic, pictorial tales

***Cue Music:** Imperial Death March*
(Darth Vader's Theme)
J.Williams,1979

2. Suffer the children

stoned on hashish upon emergence
top heavy behemoth resembles
personified improper fraction

wobbles at knees; awkward, off kilter
shift of cranium; colossal, immense
amount of weight murders endurance

three children scream
coconut caramel apples dropped
with laughter lost forever

one lady, aged to blue hair, faints
dentures fly from between dry lips
in wake of high pitched shriek of GADZOOKS!

strange bulbous sight
people wish was just humbug
trips over small boy
who proves rich in harsh expletive
a plunger dart marksman
he shoots, misses
but startles the lummox
causes its fall
bodily impact tries center post

Big Top feels tremors
as Atlas-Top trips into
ropes, pulls up pegs and
stakes that follow

confused tomfool tumbling through
support beams that crack
wood breaks to sharp
points that jab,
tear
weave-of- cloth-sky, falls
slack, makes way for
moonbeams to pour through
illuminate poles
that bend as they play the part
       of Atlas Osteoporosis
       and crumble like bone-dust
       drop the ball
       defeated under tackle
       of heavy canvas,
       which settles slowly over
       crowd that brings panic;
       muffled cries that draw

       the eyes of spectators;
          clowns,
             freaks
                animals

3. Fire parades through dead

so many perish
bug light mosquitos
under there
with airflow expired

Red Skelton's apparition tells
 jokes to a pile of charred
corpses ... much like his stage act
he does most of the laughing

government officials move in under
predetermined "no hope" orders
pin down tent; death stitch perimeter
trap all inside
as if blackbirds to be
baked alive in a pie

thick bouquet of flesh; roasted
pork, hay covered in feces and urine
on popcorn, burnt
canvas, smoldered
fur, screams as sirens
mix with laughter

and

curses that cut out
the chitter of one
marmoset flattened and killed
by the tires of a tardy fire truck
in erratic late arrival

Cue Music: Taps
General Daniel Adams Butterfield, 1862

The Last Act

Emmet Kelley's ghost appears

relives Hartford, 1944
tragic Barnum & Bailey blaze

totes spectral
water with spirit
bucket-brigade

haunts the night as Weary-Willy
sweeps the spotlight
under the rug
        once & for all ...
            the light goes out

Notes, Odds & Ends at The End by the Author

Thanks to Tim Peeler, Carter Monroe, Jim Chandler, Cait Collins RIP, Mike Maguire, Jennifer Dubin, Glen Feulner and Briana Piazza for their constant support, input and feedback.

Very special thanks to Jim Chandler, an amazing southern poet, for his support and for encouraging me to finish At The Bottom of The Big Top. Originally, At The Bottom of The Big Top was one very long poem (you will find this original text at the end of this special edition) that I'd wanted to shorten. I decided, instead, to expand it and broke it into parts which eventually became the poems in this book. Jim's encouragement kept me working on it.

Thanks to Dean Koontz for both the massive amount of respect he gives to dogs in his stories as well as in real life and also for his acknowledgment of At the Bottom of The Big Top as something he enjoyed - his having taken the time to read it and send me a note of encouragement made the world seem a bit smaller and a lot less frighteningly intangible.

Finally - massive thanks to Justice (RIP) - my old dog who was constantly with me while I was writing this book and to Dargo and Chuck the two pooches that now live with me and help me get through each day with their constant company and happiness.

* The interior art for At The Bottom Of The Big Top was taken from a flyer I drew in the early 90's to advertise a gig at a nightclub that was at one time called Bunratty's and later became The Local 186. The show featured local hardcore bands from the Boston, Massachusetts area.

* The clown on the unicycle was the cover of the original chap-book version of At The Bottom Of The Big Top. The cover pictures for this version of the book are watercolor paintings that I did in 1993. The drawing on page 40 was done in 2012.

* The picture of Emmet Kelley is a rendering of real photograph I found online while doing research about the different types of clowns, circus terminology etc. The picture is from the Hartford Circus fire of 1944 and Kelley has joined the bucket brigade to help fight the fire.

*I took the carousel Picture in Pordenone, Italy in 2008.

**Ok folks.
next you get
to read
One Dead
Marmoset**

**After that,
go peddle your papers.**

One Dead Marmoset

mad carousel horses frothing at the mouth
spinning circles around my senses
altered unclear states trick riding
spinning cogs and gears

unsuspected
circus clowns toss hatchets
seltzer bottle sprays acid
deadly joke used on bystanders and spectators
smell of vinegar and roasting pork
sizzling sounds accompany strange acrid fumes

a thousand more in polka dots, giant shoes, rubber noses
donning painted smiles over evil frowns
appear from inside of a tiny tank
its turret producing a flag marked "bang!"
they spring out storming the crowd
running forth throwing buckets of razorblade confetti

confused, ring master caught in shuffle;
sent spinning in death, arms flailing
shot to death with small clown from cannon

big top breathes
air shifting, movement inside
animals escape in the midst of confusion
elephants trample vendors peddling stale popcorn
monkeys tear apart cotton candy sellers
pawning pink fiberglass insulation

fancy horse, feathers in its bridle
gallops fast, regardless of half-naked beauty
riding bareback screaming "stop!"
with a "ninny" leaping into crowd
hooves break bones under crushing weight
pinpointed with shoes

fashioned mad doctor steel worker
in nearby covered wagon
hides blue collared MD
beer drinking con-surgeon
belching during rhinoplasty
killed the fucker right
there - on the table

time of death 512
announced with tell-tale odors
pizza and beer, cigars, women
nights debauchery finds nostrils

in tragic backlash striking
planet completes its circle
"karma" he thinks, slipping
the horn into his medical bag
imagining a cash deal
behind exotic tapestries
black market golden ticket

seeing the nurses eyes change
as scalpel flashes under shining
teeth smiling an invitation
hands fly up
clutching from either side
under blood flow
hoard of freaks now comes
side show unit
making its strike in the chaos
out from under stands
where elephant shit was swept
freaks smoked pot under there
where none could smell it
now they came out of stoned hiding
mishaps attacking with sharp blades

(everyone knows that freaks always carry knives
usually a poniard)
bearded lady bumps into ugly old man who swallows fire
her fame goes up in smoke
charred chin still smoldering
she backs into the sword swallower
who, showing off at the time, ends up gutting herself
she falls face down ass up
Joe Joe the dog faced boy becomes
Joe Joe the doggy style freak
he'd watched her swallow swords
for too many years
he was getting a piece
before the flesh got cold
jumping on without thinking
for a fuck he is impaled

one particularly miserable freak
known only as "earth"
bumbled out from under the stands last
his head the size of a medicine ball
tattooed with maps of earth
like his head was a fucking globe
using this as a gimmick
he was among the most successful tattooed man acts
the rest of his body covered in dragons
pretty ladies, unknown letters, strange symbols
meanings of which were long forgotten
never known by the person
whose body onto which they'd been stitched
forever in ink.

earth was so stoned at the time
he emerged with wobbling awkward off kilter feeling
huge head caused shifting weight
too much for him
tripped over a small child
who called him a freaky-ass-mother-fucker

pointed a gun at him, shot and missed
stumbling into center post of the big top
the whole thing began to come down
earth crashed into support beams
with a crack wood breaks
fabric above falls slack
tent poles on either side unable to support
the big top
splinter as they give

under heavy canvas
settling slowly on panicky crowd
you could hear muffled cries
spectators, mad clowns, animals, freaks etc...
so many of them died that day
under there

government officials moved in
pinned down the outside of the tent
trapping everyone inside

tarpaulin torched
all still trapped underneath
up in flames and screams
smelled of hay
animal piss
popcorn

one marmoset
run over
by fire truck
arriving too late

Eric C. Harrison is an American artist, writer and musician who lives in a drafty, but cozy, old house in a place that he calls Saltmarsh with two dogs, two turtles and a variety of small, generally unseen, furry critters. He is often approached by wild animals.

His artwork has appeared on vinyl albums of all sizes, picture discs, cd's and cassette tape covers. He has done movie story boards, covers for zines and chapbooks and has been printed in some well-known magazines such as Metal Maniacs. Eric has done designs for t shirts, buttons posters etc.

His written work includes Parallel Enigma's - a chapbook co-authored with Carter Monroe - as well as numerous poems and short prose pieces published through a wide variety of literary zines - including The Underbeat Journal, Jim Chandler's Thunder Sandwich, Tim Peeler's Third Lung Review, The-Hold, 63channels Magazine, Spitjaw Review, Beatdog Broadside & Tyrannosaurus RX. Internationally, his writing has seen print through Mass Movement zine out of Wales and Load of Noise in England. Eric was made a member of Rockzillaworld's Americana Poetry Consortium in 2002.

As a musician Eric is known for playing bass and singing in GRIEF, a Boston based doom-metal band and his current projects Bad Life-Choices (a punk band) and B9K9 (an eclectic project.) In his current projects Eric Plays guitar or drums and sings. His claim is that that when Grief broke up he began to experience sporadic transformations wherein he would become part canine and unable to play bass with paws. Apparently he has broken that barrier.

B9K9 L to R: Big D, Eric C. Harrison, Chuck-Naked

Other Books by Eric C. Harrison

Art

Blackened White
Art collection # 1

Denizens of Distraction
Art Collection # 2

Finding the Secret Sea
an experiment in spontaneity of image/word association
sketches by Eric C. Harrison with words by Mike Maguire

Writing

At The Bottom of The Big Top
A horror story told with poems.

Picture of a Paranoid
Collected poems, prose & short stories, 2002-20012

Available from Marsh Paw Press

www.marshpawpress.com

For information

Write to Eric C. Harrison
stilldiseased@aol.com

visit Marsh Paw Press on Facebook
www.facebook.com/marshpawpress

LISTEN to B9K9 for free
www.myspace.com/B9K9music

www.ingramcontent.com/pod-product-compliance
Lightning Source LLC
Chambersburg PA
CBHW071225130626
46555CB00004B/1851